The Little Rabbit Who Wanted Red Wings

by Carolyn Sherwin Bailey   Illustrated by Chris Santoro

Copyright © 1978 by Platt & Munk, Publishers. All rights reserved under International and Pan-American Copyright Conventions. Printed in the United States of America. Library of Congress Catalog Card Number: 77-84186. ISBN 0-448-46525-6 (trade); ISBN 0-448-13070-X (library) Designed by Natalie Provenzano, A Good Thing, Inc.   4 5 6 7 8 9 10

Platt & Munk, Publishers/New York
A Division of Grosset & Dunlap

Once there was a Little Rabbit who did not like himself. He had soft pink ears, bright red eyes, and a short, fluffy tail. He was a beautiful little rabbit. But he wanted to be anything except what he was.

Whenever Mr. Bushy Tail, the gray squirrel, passed by, the
Little Rabbit would say to his mother, "Oh, I wish I had a long
gray tail like Mr. Bushy Tail's."

Whenever Mr. Porcupine passed by, the Little Rabbit would say to his mother, "Oh, I wish I had a back full of bristles like Mr. Porcupine's."

And whenever Miss Puddle Duck passed by in her two red rubbers, the Little Rabbit would say to his mother, "Oh, I wish I had a pair of red rubbers like Miss Puddle Duck's."

One day, Mr. Groundhog heard the Little Rabbit wishing. Being a very wise man, Mr. Groundhog said to the Little Rabbit, "Why don't you go down to the wishing pond? If you look at yourself in the water, then turn around three times, your wish will come true."

The Little Rabbit trotted off through the woods until he came to a pool of green water lying in a low tree stump. That was the wishing pond.

Beside the wishing pond sat a small red bird, drinking
happily. As soon as the Little Rabbit saw him, he began to wish
again. "Oh," he said to himself, "I wish I had a pair of red
wings."

He looked in the wishing pond and saw his little face. He turned around three times. Then something happened. The Little Rabbit suddenly felt as if he were cutting teeth in his shoulders. His wings were coming through.

All the rest of the day, the Little Rabbit sat by the wishing pond, waiting joyfully while his wings grew. Just before sundown, he started home to show his mother the beautiful pair of red wings.

It was dark when the Little Rabbit reached home. He knocked excitedly on the door. His mother opened it immediately, but just as quickly she shut it. For she most certainly did not know a little rabbit with red wings.

The Little Rabbit had no choice but to go looking for a place to spend the night. Shortly, he came upon Mr. Bushy Tail's house. He rapped on the door and said, "Please, Mr. Bushy Tail, may I sleep in your house tonight?" But as soon as Mr. Bushy Tail saw the strange rabbit, he slammed the door shut.

The Little Rabbit went on until he came to Miss Puddle
Duck's nest by the marsh. "Please, Miss Puddle Duck," he said,
"may I sleep in your nest tonight?"

Miss Puddle Duck poked her head out of the nest just a little
way. "No, no, no," she said. "Go away." For she, too, did not
know such an odd rabbit.

The Little Rabbit went on and on until he came to Mr. Groundhog's hole. The wise Mr. Groundhog recognized him at once and let him sleep in the hole. But the hole had beechnuts spread all over it. And while that pleased Mr. Groundhog endlessly, it made the Little Rabbit very uncomfortable. He slept terribly.

By morning the Little Rabbit was in despair. Mr. Groundhog, knowing the time was right, went to his friend.

"Do you still want your red wings?" asked Mr. Groundhog.

"Oh, no," said the Little Rabbit.

"Well, then," said Mr. Groundhog, "why don't you go down to the wishing pond and wish them off again?"

The Little Rabbit scampered off to the wishing pond. He looked at his face in it, turned around three times, and then watched his red wings shrink away to nothing at all.

Then the Little Rabbit went right home to his mother. She was delighted to see the little rabbit she knew and loved. And he, at last, was happy to be that rabbit.